Usborne
Aesop's
Stories
for Little
Children

Contents

The Fox and the Crow

It was a warm
summer's day
and Fox was
feeling hungry.

"The bees have honey,"
he sighed.
"Rabbit has a carrot.
What is there for me?"

6

Then, he smelled something delicious.
He looked up, licking his lips.

High in the
treetops sat Crow...

8

...with a big chunk of crumbly
yellow cheese in her beak.

9

Fox closed his eyes and sniffed hungrily.
But the cheese was far out of reach.

"What can I do?"
He gave a crafty smile.

Fox cleared his throat loudly.

"Oh beautiful Crow!"
he began.

12

Crow looked down, startled.

No one had ever
called her **beautiful** before.

"What sleek, shining feathers
you have! What a fine
midnight black they are!"

Crow's beak was too full to reply.
But she fluttered her wings proudly.

15

Crow listened
happily as Fox
went on.

"Is your singing voice as beautiful as your feathers?" he sighed.

I wish you would sing to me.

17

Crow hopped
shyly from foot
to foot.

18

"Please sing!" begged Fox.

Pleeease!

Crow couldn't resist.

She stretched her beak wide and screeched.

Caw! Caw!

Down tumbled the cheese...

21

SNAP!

...straight into Fox's
waiting jaws.

Give it back!

Crow flapped furiously.

"Hey!" she snapped.
　　"That is MY cheese!"

24

Fox gulped it down and gave a broad, cheesy grin.

"Not any more," he laughed.

That was delicious!

Fox padded away, chuckling.

Crow was cross but she
had learned her lesson.

26

Don't be fooled by flattery.

The Hare and the Tortoise

Harry Hare
loved to run.

He loved the feel of the wind in his ears...

...he loved
ZOOming
past other animals...

...and he loved telling everyone how **absolutely amazingly** fast he was.

31

One day, Harry was boasting to Tom Tortoise.
"I could beat anyone in a race," he bragged.

"Really?" said Tom, getting to his feet.
"Well, why don't you race me?"

Ha ha ha.

Harry exploded with laughter.
"**You?**" he snorted. "Tommy Slowcoach?"

Tom nodded. "Why not?" he insisted.
"Are you worried about losing?"

"Of course not," giggled Harry.
"It'll be a laugh."

On the day of the race, Harry got up before dawn.
He couldn't wait to start racing...

...so he
went for a
run by himself.

Tom Tortoise, on the other hand, got up at his usual time and had his usual breakfast...

...four cherry buns and a big pot of tea.

Lots of animals came
to watch the start.

Harry chatted happily
to his fans.

Tom's friends
looked worried.
"Do you want to call it off?"
asked Squirrel.
"Harry's very fast, you know."

"Take your places,"
called old Brown Owl.

Harry tapped a toe impatiently
while Tom crawled over.

Hurry up!

Start

Owl raised a red flag.

On your marks...

Get set...

GO!

Harry zoomed
into the distance
as Tom plodded
slowly over
the line.

Halfway around the course, Harry paused.
Tom was nowhere in sight.

"Winning will be a piece of cake," he thought.

Mmm, cake...

His tummy rumbled.
He had been too
busy to bother
with breakfast.

"I'm so far ahead, it won't matter if I stop for a minute."

He flung himself down in the shade, picked up an apple and began to munch.

41

Then – aaaaaah – he yawned.
The grass was very soft
and he had been up very early.

"I'll just shut my
eyes for a moment,"
he mumbled.

Seconds later, there was a faint snore.
Harry was fast asleep.

Meanwhile, Tom plodded patiently on.

Hours passed.

Slowly but surely,

step by tiny

tortoise step...

Come on, Tom!

You can do it!

...the finish line drew closer.

Harry woke with a start.
How long had he been asleep?

46

He sprang to his feet and raced off.
There was the finish line.
Already he could hear a distant roar...

Hurrah!

"They're cheering
for me," he chuckled.

But what was that?

A small shape was creeping up to the finish.

"Oh no!" Harry gasped, putting on an extra burst of speed.

Look, it's Harry!

Where have you been?

He dived over the line... **too late!**

Tom Tortoise had won –
and he wasn't even out of breath.

Slow and steady wins the race.

The Ant
and the
Grasshopper

It was a glorious summer's day.
Grasshopper chirruped and
sang sunny songs.

Ant was too busy to sing.
He huffed...
...and he puffed...
...and he g-r-o-a-n-e-d...

as he hauled food away
to his winter store.

Grasshopper smiled and
lay back on a leaf, drowsy
and dozing in the sun.

After a while, he called out to Ant,
"You're working too hard!"

"I have to,"
Ant panted.
"There's so much to do."

59

"I must collect
all this food
for the winter."

60

"But winter is ages away,"
said Grasshopper.

"Enjoy the sunshine
with me while you can!"

"Winter may seem ages away," Ant replied,
"but it will come all too swiftly."

"If you don't work now...

...why, when the sun has long gone and the Earth
is sleeping, you will be cold and hungry."

Grasshopper laughed and sang on.

Ant huffed...
and he puffed...
and carried more corn.

Sure enough, winter crept over the Earth.
Trees stood bare against the bleak sky.
Snow dusted the fields.

Tucked up snug in his
little home, Ant looked at
his food store and smiled.

He had boxes galore, plenty to keep him fed
until the spring buds blossomed.

Outside, in a blustery gale,
Grasshopper scrunched himself up,
trying to shelter behind a leaf.

But the wind blew through his
trembling body, however tightly he curled.
His tummy ached with hunger.

At last, he fought through the wind to Ant's house. "Ant! Help!" Grasshopper shouted.

Ant poked his head outside his door.

72

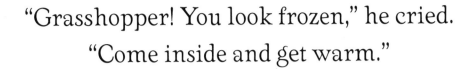

"Grasshopper! You look frozen," he cried.
"Come inside and get warm."

"Thaw out by the stove," said Ant, "and I'll make supper."

74

Grasshopper beamed.
He could almost taste
the toasted corn already.

"Thank you, Ant. I promise,
next summer, I'll work too!"

It's best to be prepared.

The Greedy Dog

Dog was padding along,
dreaming about dinner.

Mmmm...

He had already polished off a slice of steak,
half a ham and a whole string of sausages.

"What can I eat next?" he wondered.

79

Eventually he came to a town.
It was market day...

...and something smelled **delicious.**

Dog sniffed happily
and trotted closer.

What's that?

"Ooh, look at that big, juicy bone!" he drooled, his tongue hanging out in delight.

"I've **got** to have it!"

The butcher was busy selling sausages.
No one noticed greedy Dog.

Slowly,
silently,
he crept
closer...

...and closer.

Hey!

Snap!

His teeth closed
around the bone.

And he sprinted
away before anyone
could stop him.

85

Soon, the town
was far behind.

I'm so clever.

Dog wagged his tail with satisfaction.

"Now I have my bone to eat," he thought.
"I just need something to drink."

His path ran past
a rippling river.

"That water
looks good,"
thought Dog.

Dog padded over to the water's edge. He peered down...

...and saw another dog gazing back at him.

What was more, the other dog had a bone too!

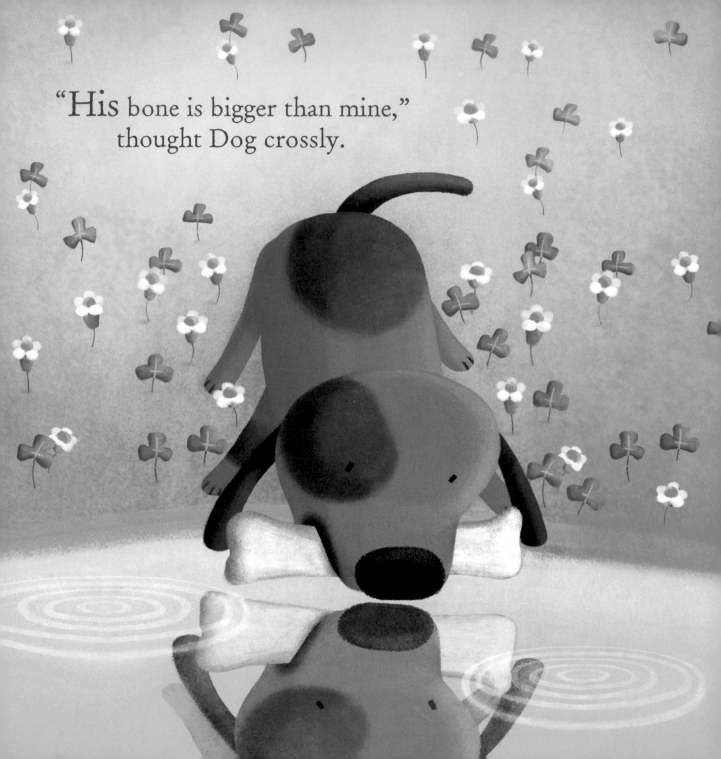

"His bone is bigger than mine,"
thought Dog crossly.

"It's not fair!
His bone looks
so big and juicy."

"I've **got** to have it!

How can I make
him drop it?"

Dog bared his sharp, white teeth
and let out a fierce growl.

Grrr!

The dog in the water growled back just as fiercely.

Grrr!

Dog wasn't going to give up. He raised his hackles and barked furiously.

"Uh-oh!" His big, beautiful bone
dropped out of his mouth and fell...

Splosh!

...into the river.

Ripples spread
across the surface.

The other dog
vanished...

...and so did Dog's bone.

96

"Nooo!" whined Dog. He reached after it, but the water was too deep.

Now I have nothing.

His bone had sunk without a trace.

Too late Dog realized...
there was no dog in the water.

And there was no
other bone.

98

He had been jealous of his own reflection!

Be happy with what you have.

The Lion and the Mouse

One long, hot afternoon, Lion
was snoozing in the shade.

102

103

When, pitter-patter, pitter-patter... swish-swish...

...a little tail brushed
the tip of his nose.

Aaaaaa–choooooooooooooo!!! sneezed Lion.

He awoke with a start.

"How dare you disturb me!"
Lion snarled at a terrified mouse.

"I'm s-so sorry,"
stammered the mouse.
"I didn't mean to...
I didn't realize..."

"Do you know what I do to those who wake me?" Lion roared.

I eat them up!

"Please don't eat me," begged the mouse.

"Spare my life today and maybe, one day, I'll save yours."

"YOU?" scoffed Lion. "What could YOU ever do to help me? Run along, little mouse. I'm laughing too much to eat you."

And the mouse ran - as fast as she could.

The very next day, Lion walked straight into a hunter's trap.

He roared and he struggled, but the more he struggled, the tighter the trap became.

"I'm stuck," he realized. "I'll never get out!"

But the little mouse heard his cries.

She rushed to his side.
"Don't worry," she squeaked.
"I've come to save you."

"What can you do?" groaned Lion.
"You're much too small to help me."

The mouse ignored him, and set to work.
She nibbled and gnawed at the gnarly old ropes.

She nibbled all day and all night.

At last, as the sun rose in the
sky, Lion was free once more.

"You saved me!" said Lion, holding her gently in his paw.
"I was wrong to laugh at you, little mouse."

120

"I see size doesn't matter, after all."

Little friends can be great friends.

The Fox and the Stork

Fox and Stork were the best of friends...

...well, most
of the time.

Fox LOVED playing tricks –
whether his friends enjoyed them or not.

One day, Fox dreamed up a brand new trick...

This will be fun!

...a trick that he could play over dinner.

All afternoon,
Fox simmered
and stirred.

Mmmmmm...

Delicious smells wafted through the woods.

When Stork arrived,
Fox ladled spoonfuls of
steaming soup into dishes –

132

wide, flat dishes.

Stork watched hungrily.

133

She poked and
she pecked...

...but she couldn't fit
her beak into the dish.

However hard she
tried, she couldn't
swallow a drop.

Fox smirked and slurped his soup.
He finished every last drop.

Not hungry?
I'll eat yours!

Stork scowled.
"It's time to teach
Fox a lesson,"
she thought.

The next day, Stork invited Fox to dinner.

Once again, the smell of simmering soup filled the air.

Fox licked his lips as he walked through the woods.

139

Fox watched eagerly while Stork ladled the steaming soup into jars –

tall,
thin
jars.

Poor Fox!

He squashed and
he squeezed...

...but he couldn't fit
his nose into the jar.

However hard he tried, he couldn't swallow a drop.

Stork smiled and
sipped her soup.

Fox folded his arms in a huff.

"That was a **rotten** trick!" he growled.

"You tricked me first," Stork pointed out quietly.

Let's be friends again.

Fox and Stork parted best friends once more.

"I'm sorry," called Fox.
"I won't play any more tricks...

...until next time!"

Treat others as you would
like them to treat you.

The Tortoise and the Eagle

It was a perfect day in the orchard.

The sun shone and the wind whispered softly in the trees.

150

But Tortoise wasn't happy.

Oh! It's just terrible being a tortoise.

His friends were puzzled.
"Why are you so glum?" they asked.

"You have a lovely log to sit on,
yummy apples to eat, and
a very shiny shell."

But Tortoise just
mumbled and
grumbled.

Oh, it's terrible being me.

All day long,
he watched an
eagle in the sky.

She swooped down low...

...and soared up high.

Her golden feathers
shimmered in the sun.

Tortoise watched in wonder.

I wish I could fly like that.

So he decided to try.

He closed his eyes, gritted his teeth, flapped his arms and hopped.

But he couldn't get into the sky.

"I know," said Tortoise,
"I need to start up high."
He clambered onto a rock...

jumped into
the air...

...and landed splosh
on the soggy grass.

OOF!

"I know," he said, again.
"I need to start up higher."
So he climbed a tree...

158

flung himself off...

...and landed splat
in a muddy puddle.

URRGH!

He called to the eagle up above.

Eagle! Eagle! Flying so high.

Won't you take me into the sky?

The golden bird
swooped down
from the clouds.

"Little tortoise," she
squawked, "why do
you wish to fly?"

Tortoise puffed up his
chest and answered proudly.
"So I can be just like you."

"I'll give you my log to rest on," said Tortoise. "And you can have my juicy apples to eat."

"Very well," said the eagle.
"I will take you into the sky."

The eagle grasped Tortoise in her claws.

She flapped her
enormous wings.

Up and up they rose...
up through the clouds...

...into the bright blue sky.

The wind tickled Tortoise's face.
"I'm flying," he laughed.

They rose higher
and higher.
Below them, the
trees looked tiny.

The tortoise gazed at the ground.
It was a **very** long way down.

166

His head felt dizzy.
His tummy went wobbly.
And then he started to cry.

Eagle! Eagle! Take me down!
I don't like it
up in the sky!

The eagle carried the tortoise
back to the ground.

"Little tortoise," she said.
"You have no feathers. You have no wings."

"You are not made for flying.
Keep your apples and your log.
Be a tortoise and be happy."

Tortoise watched the eagle
soar up and away.

He munched his apples.
He sat on his log. And he
no longer wanted to fly.

170

It's terrific being a tortoise.

Be happy with who you are.

The Sun and the Wind

It was a fine summer's day.
The Sun beamed down. He was pleased
to see everyone enjoying themselves.

"Look at me!"
he said, smiling.

"Huh," huffed the Wind, grumpily.
"Listen to me."

He blew a sudden squall,
whipping up the waves,
snatching sunhats and
upending umbrellas.

176

"Stop," said the Sun. "Those people want to be warm."

He shone so brightly, ice creams began to drip.

"Oops," he laughed.
"I'm too strong."

179

"But I'm stronger," boasted the Wind,
blowing dark storm clouds across the sky.

"He needs to be taught a lesson," the Sun thought.

"I bet I can," roared the Wind.
Puffing out his cheeks,
he blew a great gust.

The birds turned somersaults in the air...

...and the man nearly
fell over backwards.

"That won't work," laughed
the Sun. "Look, he's cold.
He's buttoning his coat."

The Wind blew harder still.

The man put up his hood, and pulled his coat tighter.

The Wind blew his hardest, and the man hurried into a shelter. "I give up," groaned the Wind, exhausted.

"My turn," said the Sun.
The Wind was still.

The man looked out.

The Sun shone down gently,
and the birds started singing again.

The man pulled back his hood.
"He's warm now," said the Sun.

The Sun shone with all his might.

The man smiled and unbuttoned his coat.

When he reached the beach, he took it off altogether.

"I win!" laughed the Sun.

193

The Wind blew away in a huff, leaving the man
to bask in glorious golden sunshine.

Gentleness is better than force.

The
Town Mouse
and the
Country Mouse

In among the waving grasses...

...lay a little brown country mouse, fast asleep.
His name was Pipin.

He dreamed of crunchy seeds
and juicy red strawberries.

Every evening Pipin
pattered home...

...to his little house
in the leafy hedge.

Until, one cold winter's day, there was
a RAT-A-TAT-TAT at his door.

"Pipin!" cried a voice.
It was Toby Town Mouse, come to stay.

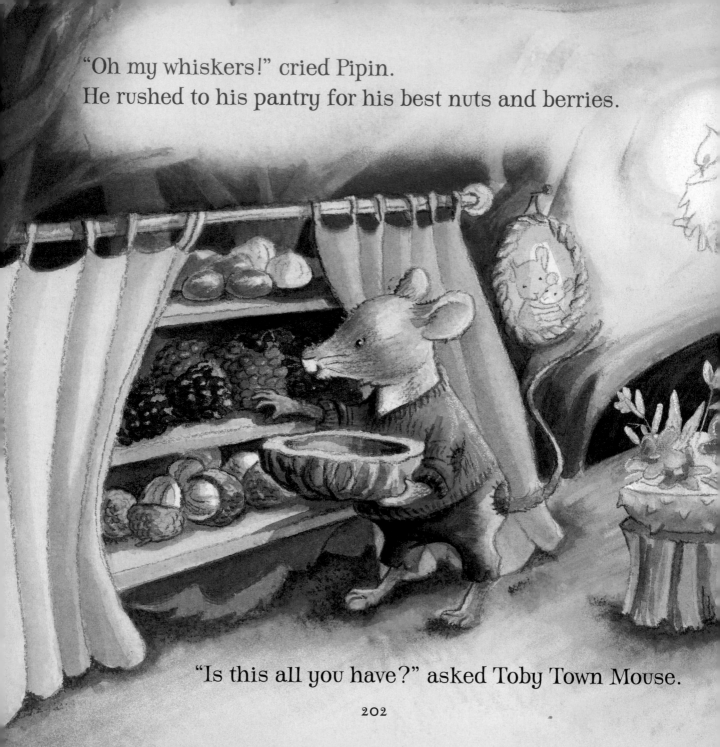

"Oh my whiskers!" cried Pipin.
He rushed to his pantry for his best nuts and berries.

"Is this all you have?" asked Toby Town Mouse.

202

"In town we eat like kings.
I think you'd better come and stay with me."

The mice scampered to the station
early next morning.

The train trundled in with
a snort and a shriek.

"It's HUGE!" gasped Pipin.
"It's like a big red **beast**."

They wriggled inside a man's
green bag and were lifted aboard. Then...

Chugga-chugga-chugga. Choo! Choo!
They were off!

Pipin gazed out of the window,
at trees waving their branches.

Soon there were no trees at all –
just tall buildings that touched the sky.

"At last!" cried Toby, sniffing the air. "We're here!"

Hurry up, Pipin!

They ran out of the station
onto a busy street.

"Help!" squeaked Pipin, dodging
in and out of stamping feet.

"This is it," said Toby, proudly pointing his paw. "My house."
They crept through a crack under the blue front door.

Toby led Pipin down under the floor,
up secret stairs behind the walls...

...and into a splendid dining room.

The mice munched
and crunched...

and scooped cream
with their paws...

...until they were
perfectly full.

They woke with a start as the table shook.

"MY dinner time!" purred the kitchen cat.

Mmmmm...
juicy little mice.

"Run!" squeaked Toby.

The mice darted
this way
and that.

Pounce! Pounce!
went the hungry cat.

She swiped at Pipin
with sharp, pointy claws.

Quick, Pipin! Into this hole.

Pipin ran.
    The cat leaped...

...and missed.
    "Curses!" she hissed.

"Oh my whiskers," said Pipin, mopping his brow.
"I want to go home."

Oh! Why?

This town life is too much for me.

Toby took Pipin to the station
and waved goodbye.

Pipin gazed again
as tall buildings
flashed past his eyes.

In the starry dark, Pipin finally
reached his hedge.

He sniffed the cold, sweet air and smiled.

Then he snuggled down
in his soft, mossy bed.
"This is the life for me," he said.

Each to their own.

About Aesop

People think the stories in this book were written by a man named Aesop, who lived in Greece around 2,500 years ago. No real proof survives, but some ancient writers do talk about a man named Aesop.

These writers say that Aesop started
life as a slave. He was ugly but clever,
and very good at telling stories.
His tales were usually about animals
or objects, and always contained a 'moral'
or lesson about how to behave.

Eventually, Aesop's master was so impressed
by the stories that he gave Aesop his
freedom. Aesop then went on to work for
a king, using his tales to help people
understand each other.

Today, the stories – often known as Aesop's fables – are popular all over the world, and many of the morals have become well-known sayings.

Edited by Rosie Dickins and Lesley Sims

Designed by Laura Wood and Caroline Spatz

Additional illustrations: Antonia Miller
Digital manipulation: John Russell

First published in 2014 by Usborne Publishing Ltd.,
Usborne House, 83–85 Saffron Hill, London EC1N 8RT, England.
www.usborne.com
Copyright © 2014, 2012, 2009, 2008, 2007 Usborne Publishing Ltd.